DISNEY·PIXAR

MONSTERS, INC.

Novelization

Adapted by Kiki Thorpe

Designed by Disney's Global Design Group

PUFFIN BOOKS

PUFFIN BOOKS

Published by the Penguin Group
Penguin Books Ltd, 80 Strand, London WC2R 0RL, England
Penguin Putnam Inc., 375 Hudson Street, New York, New York 10014, USA
Penguin Books Australia Ltd, 250 Camberwell Road, Camberwell,
Victoria 3124, Australia
Penguin Books Canada Ltd, 10 Alcorn Avenue, Toronto, Ontario, Canada M4V 3B2
Penguin Books India (P) Ltd, 11 Community Centre, Panchsheel Park,
New Delhi – 110 017, India
Penguin Books (NZ) Ltd, Cnr Rosedale and Airborne Roads, Albany,
Auckland, New Zealand
Penguin Books (South Africa) (Pty) Ltd, 24 Sturdee Avenue,
Rosebank 2196, South Africa

Penguin Books Ltd, Registered Offices: 80 Strand, London WC2R 0RL, England

www.penguin.com

First published in the USA by Random House, Inc. and in Canada by Random House of
Canada Limited in conjunction with Disney Enterprises, Inc. 2001
Published in the UK in Puffin Books 2002
1

Text copyright © Disney Enterprises, Inc./Pixar Animation Studios, 2001
All rights reserved

Set in 14.5 on 18pt Times Ten Roman

Made and printed in England by Clays Ltd, St Ives plc

British Library Cataloguing in Publication Data
A CIP catalogue record for this book is available from the British Library

ISBN 0–141–31431–1

CHAPTER 1

Moonlight streamed through the bed-room window, making spooky shadows on the bed. Tucked beneath the covers, a little boy was sound asleep.

Creeeeak. The boy's closet door slowly opened.

The sound startled the boy awake. He sat up and glanced nervously around. But the room was empty. The boy lay back down and snuggled into his pillow.

Creeeeak. The floorboards groaned as something moved across the room.

The boy peered into the darkness. Suddenly his eyes grew round with fright.

A monstrous tentacle was slithering out of the door of his closet! Terrified, the boy squeezed his eyes shut. But when he looked again, he saw there was no tentacle after all. It was just the sleeve of his shirt hanging out of the closet door. Sighing with relief, the boy settled back under the covers.

Just then a menacing shadow slipped across the room.

Beneath the boy's bed, two evil eyes peered out of the darkness.

The boy was wide awake now, huddled under the bedcovers and shaking with fear. From under the bed a monster rose. Its dark, hulking form blocked the moonlight as it loomed over the small child. Raising two ghastly arms, the monster opened its mouth. But before it could let out its bloodcurdling roar, the terrified boy released a piercing scream.

The startled monster yelled and stepped on a football. It shot out from under the monster's foot, hit the wall, and flew back at the monster's head. *'Oomph!'* it grunted. Then the monster tripped on some toys and ran into a chest of drawers, which fell over and landed on its foot.

Suddenly the lights in the room came on, and the little boy flopped forward on the bed like a puppet.

'Simulation terminated. Simulation terminated,' said a computerized voice. One of the walls of the bedroom began to rise into the air. The bedroom wasn't really a bedroom at all – it was a practice room made to *look* like a real bedroom!

The little boy actually *was* a puppet. The simulated bedroom was part of a training programme at the Monsters, Inc. factory. Bile, the monster in the bedroom, was being tested on his ability to scare.

Blinking in the bright lights, Bile growled awkwardly at the limp puppet a few more times.

Just beyond the bedroom set, a

dragon-like monster named Ms Flint watched this action being replayed on several TV monitors. The monitors showed the now uncomfortable Bile from different angles.

Ms Flint sighed. 'All right, Mr Bile,' she said.

Bile stopped growling. 'Uh, my friends call me Phlegm,' he told her.

'*Mr Bile,* can you tell me what you did wrong?' she asked.

'Fell down?' Bile said uncertainly.

'Can anyone tell me what Mr Bile did wrong?' Ms Flint demanded, turning to look at a row of monsters who had been watching Bile practise his scaring technique.

The monsters shifted uneasily in their seats. None of them had any idea what the answer to the question might be. Finally one monster opened his mouth as if to answer Ms Flint's question, but then he only coughed.

Ms Flint put her scaly head down on

her desk and sighed with frustration. Turning this group of pathetic recruits into Scarers was no easy task.

'Let's take a look at the tape.' She pointed to one of the TV monitors. On the screen, Bile sneaked once again into the bedroom. But this time the image froze on the closet door.

'There! See?' said Ms Flint. 'The door. You left it wide open.'

'Ohhhh,' said the monster recruits.

'Leaving a door open is the worst mistake any employee can make, because . . .' Ms Flint paused to wait for the answer.

'It could let in a draught?' Bile answered hesitantly.

'It could let in a *child*!' boomed a voice from the back of the room.

'Oh, Mr Waternoose!' Ms Flint cried in surprise as a stout, crab-like monster in a waistcoat and bow tie scuttled forward.

Bile and the other recruits gasped. They hadn't known that Henry J.

Waternoose, the CEO of Monsters, Inc., was watching!

Waternoose glared at the wimpy recruits with all five of his beady eyes.

'There is nothing more toxic or deadly than a human child,' he said dramatically. 'A single touch could kill you! Leave a door open, and a child could walk right into this factory – right into the monster world.' The monsters gulped. Children's screams powered most of the city of Monstropolis, but they were considered a very dangerous source of energy.

One terrified recruit jumped into the lap of the monster sitting next to him. 'I won't go in a kid's room. You can't make me!'

Waternoose held up a yellow canister. 'You're going in there because we need this.' He uncorked the canister and an earsplitting scream pierced the air. As it did, the lights in the room glowed white-hot, lit up by the power of the scream. The recruits cringed.

Waternoose looked around the room in frustration. Human children were getting harder and harder to scare. Monstropolis was in the middle of an energy crisis. Right now, Monsters, Inc. supplied most of the scream energy for the city. But if he didn't get some good Scarers soon, his company might go out of business!

'Our city is counting on you to collect those children's screams – without screams we have no power,' he told the recruits. 'I need Scarers who are confident, tenacious, tough, intimidating. I need Scarers like . . . James P. Sullivan!'

CHAPTER 2

A giant foot hit the floor with a thud. Huge hairy blue hands cracked their knuckles. A fierce pair of eyes squinted. Two sets of sharp, gleaming teeth parted to release a ferocious roar. James P. Sullivan was ready to start his day.

Eight feet tall, blue with purple spots and sharp horns, James P. Sullivan was also known as Sulley – and he was the best Scarer in the business. There was hardly a child in the world he couldn't scare. But even the scariest monster in the world had to stay in shape.

He dropped to the floor and began to

do push-ups. Next to him, a small, round, green monster with a single large eye in the middle of his face cheered him on.

Mike Wazowski was Sulley's best friend and room-mate. He was also the personal assistant to the top Scarer at Monsters, Inc. Mike coached his big friend through his monster workout. 'Scary feet! Scary feet!' he cried as Sulley ran in place. 'The kid's awake!' Sulley dropped to the floor. 'Scary feet! Scar– the kid's asleep!' Sulley popped back up.

In their living-room, Sulley pushed a huge pile of furniture across the floor.

'GRRR,' Sulley growled.

In the bathroom, Sulley brushed his giant teeth. Mike stood on Sulley's arm, coaching away. 'Fight that plaque! Fight that plaque! Scary monsters don't have plaque!' he cried. Mike wanted to be sure his friend was in tip-top shape for a day of scaring. They hoped Sulley would break the all-time scare record that day.

Soon the two friends were ready for a day on the job at Monsters, Inc. They stepped out of their apartment building, and Mike walked straight over to a shiny new convertible parked at the kerb.

'OK, Sulley, hop on in!' he said cheerfully.

But Sulley knew all about the energy crisis. He didn't want to waste any scream energy by driving. 'Nope. Uh-uh,' he told Mike, grabbing his friend's skinny arm and starting to drag him along the street. 'There's a scream shortage. We're walking.'

'Walking? No, no, no! My car needs to be driven!' Mike cried. But he was no match for his big blue friend, who continued to pull him down the pavement.

'Hey, genius, you want to know why I bought the car?' Mike asked sarcastically as they walked along.

'Not really,' Sulley said.

'To drive it!' Mike answered anyway.

'Give it a rest, will ya, butterball?

C'mon, you could use the exercise,' Sulley teased his round pal.

'*I* could use the exercise? Look at *you*! You have your own climate,' Mike shot back.

The two passed a group of monster kids who were skipping – using one kid's tongue as the rope!

'Morning, Mike! Morning, Sulley!' a monster kid called.

'Morning, kids. How're you doing?' Sulley replied, waving.

'Bye, Mike. Bye, Thulley,' the kid with a skipping rope for a tongue called after them.

Even though it was early in the morning, the streets of Monstropolis were bustling. A street-cleaning monster swept rubbish into a small pile. Opening his large mouth, he dumped the rubbish inside and began to chew.

Nearby, a monster reading a newspaper ambled along the street. Suddenly he sneezed. '*Ah-CHOO!*' Fire shot from his nose and mouth. The newspaper quickly went up in flames. 'Aw, nuts,' he said.

A monster grocer used his many tentacles to arrange his fruit stand. 'Hey, fellas! I hear somebody's close to breaking the all-time scare record,' he said to Mike and Sulley as they walked past.

'Just trying to make sure there's enough scream to go around,' Sulley replied with a smile.

As Mike and Sulley continued down the street, a large, blob-like monster oozed by them on the pavement and accidentally crossed a grating. *'Ayyyy!'* he cried as his body began to pour through the many little holes.

At the crossing, Mike and Sulley paused to wait for the light. A giant monster with legs the size of tree trunks stood next to them.

'Hey, Ted! Good morning,' Sulley said to the giant monster.

'ROARRRRR!' Ted replied.

The traffic sign changed from DON'T

STALK to STALK, and the three monsters crossed the street.

'See that, Mikey? Ted's walking to work,' Sulley cheerfully pointed out.

'Big deal,' Mike grumbled. 'The guy takes five steps and he's there.'

The lobby of the Monsters, Inc. headquarters was a whirlwind of activity. Tall, small, scaly, furry, slippery and slimy – monsters of every shape and size scurried this way and that. Several called out greetings as Sulley and Mike walked through the door.

'Morning, Sulley!'

'Hey, it's the Sullster!'

'How are you doing, big guy?'

Sulley was popular at Monsters, Inc. And no wonder! Along one wall of the lobby, a line of framed photographs featured the Scarer of the Month. Sulley's picture was in every frame. He'd won the award every month for the past three years!

At the reception desk, Mike paused. 'Oh, Schmoopsie-Poo,' he called sweetly to the receptionist.

Celia, the receptionist, turned around – and so did the writhing snakes growing out of her head! When Celia saw that it was Mike, she smiled and batted the lashes of her one eye.

'Happy birthday,' Mike told her.

'Oh, Googly-Woogly, you remembered!' Celia cried. She leaned forward and rubbed Mike's round head. Her snakes sighed happily. Sulley stood there awkwardly, watching the couple flirt.

'So, are we going anywhere special tonight?' Celia asked Mike.

'I just got us into a little place called Harryhausen's,' Mike told her. Celia and her snakes gasped in delight. Harryhausen's was one of the fanciest restaurants in Monstropolis! 'I'll see you at 5:01, and not a minute later,' Mike said, waving good-bye to his sweetheart as he and Sulley headed off to work.

CHAPTER 3

In the locker-room at Monsters, Inc., Scarers and their assistants were getting ready for a day on the job. Sulley polished his horns, while Mike popped a contact lens the size of a hubcap into his eye.

Without warning, the door of Mike's locker suddenly slammed shut. Mike gasped in surprise.

He opened the locker door. Again it shut with a bang. 'What the...?'

Suddenly a large, purple, lizard-like monster appeared, seemingly out of nowhere! 'Wazowski!' he hissed, showing rows of sharp teeth.

'*Ahhhhh!*' Mike screamed, leaping back from the locker.

The scaly monster, Randall, chuckled. He'd been blending in with Mike's locker like a chameleon. 'Whaddya know?' he said nastily. 'It scares little kids *and* little monsters.'

'Hey, Randall. Save it for the Scare Floor, will ya?' Sulley said, coming to his friend's rescue.

Randall fixed Sulley with an evil stare. He began to wave his arms like a karate fighter. 'I'm in the zone today, Sullivan – going to be doing some serious scaring,' he said threateningly, 'putting up some big numbers.' At Monsters, Inc., Randall was the second-best Scarer, next to Sulley. He was determined to be the *best*.

But not if Mike and Sulley could help it. Mike put a thin green arm around his pal. 'Wow, Randall, that's great,' he said. 'That should make it even more humiliating when *we* break the record first.'

Randall put a hand to his ear. 'Shhh,' he said. 'Do you hear that?' He paused. 'It's the winds of change.' Snickering to himself, he sauntered out of the room.

'What a creep!' Mike snapped as soon as Randall was gone. He turned to Sulley. 'One of these days, I am really... gonna let you teach that guy a lesson.'

On his way to the station where he and Sulley worked, Mike stopped to pick up his paperwork. 'Good morning, Roz, my succulent little garden snail, and who would we be scaring today?' he said to the dispatch manager.

'Wazowski,' the slug-like monster replied, 'you didn't file your paperwork last night.'

'Oh, that darn paperwork,' Mike said. 'Wouldn't it be easier if it all just blew away?'

Roz leaned in close to Mike. 'Don't let it happen again,' she said threateningly.

'Yes, well, I'll try to be less careless,' Mike answered as he backed away nervously.

'I'm watching you, Wazowski – always watching.'

'Ooh, she's nuts,' Mike muttered to himself as he walked toward the Scare Floor. 'Slug.'

'All Scare Floors are now active,' Celia announced over the loudspeaker. 'Assistants, please report to your stations.'

Mike and the other assistants got to work preparing their stations. The Scare Floor was the most important part of Monsters, Inc. It was where the Scarers did their work. When an assistant inserted a special card key into a slot, a door dropped into the station. These doors opened to the human world – right into children's closets. Monsters, Inc. had one door for every child in the world. A Scarer's job was to pop through one of these doors, frighten a child, and exit through the door back into the monster world. Meanwhile, special mechanisms attached to the closet doors collected the kids' screams in yellow canisters.

'OK, people,' a floor manager announced. 'We've got Scarers coming out!'

From the end of the hall, a line of scary monsters slowly emerged out of the shadows. They lined up in front of their doors. Their assistants lined up behind them. On the wall above them, a large scoreboard showed the scream totals: Sulley was in first place, Randall in second.

The Scarers geared up. Sulley cracked his knuckles. Another monster flexed his claws like a cat. An assistant handed a ferocious set of teeth to a monster with a shrunken, toothless mouth. The monster slid the choppers into place, then snapped his mouth open and closed.

Fungus, Randall's assistant, yanked

a patterned backdrop down behind Randall. Randall suddenly changed colours, blending in with the wood pattern. Fungus pulled down a second background, this time decorated with a sky pattern. Randall quickly turned bright blue to match.

A bald-headed monster put a finger in his mouth and blew hard. A line of spikes popped out of his head. An assistant brushed another monster's sharp teeth with a giant toothbrush. A monster with no eyes grabbed a handful of eyeballs and popped them into his face.

Then the floor manager began the countdown. The Scarers took their places.

Sulley looked over at Randall. 'Hey,' he said, trying to be a good sport, 'may the best monster win.'

'I plan to,' Randall sneered, and crouched into a starting position.

CHAPTER 4

'Five . . . four . . . three . . . two . . . one.'

A horn blared. A sign suddenly flashed on: SCARE.

All down the line, monsters sprang forward. Sulley shot through his door. With a tremendous growl, Randall did the same. The scaring had begun.

From behind the doors came the shrill sound of children screaming. The yellow scream canisters began to fill up. As soon as one can was full, an assistant replaced it.

Sulley popped back through the door and checked the scoreboard. He was still

21

in the lead. He grinned. 'Oh, I'm feeling good today, Mikey!' he said.

As Mike and Sulley watched, Sulley's score grew higher.

'Attaboy!' Mike cheered. 'Another door coming right up!' He quickly inserted a card key, and another child's door dropped into Sulley's slot.

Just then Randall emerged from his door. He looked at the scoreboard and growled angrily when he saw that Sulley was still ahead.

'You're still behind, Randall,' Fungus said. 'Perhaps I should realign the scream intake valve – '

'Just get me another door!' Randall said through clenched teeth.

'Waaaah!' Fungus cried as he hurried to get a door.

All across the Scare Floor, monsters were dashing in and out of doors. Lights flashed. Screams echoed. Canisters filled with screams tumbled into holders.

Waternoose walked on to the floor to

check out the work. 'Well, Jerry, what's the damage so far?' he asked the manager.

'We may actually make our quota today, sir,' the manager replied.

Suddenly a monster burst through his door, screaming. He slammed the door behind him, then leaned against it, gasping for breath. He was sweating; his eyes rolled in terror. The scream canister attached to his door fell down empty.

'What happened?' his assistant asked.

'The kid almost touched me! She got *this* close to me!' the monster cried in a panicked voice.

The assistant looked down at his paperwork. 'She wasn't scared of you?' he asked in disbelief. 'She was only six!'

The monster began to cry. 'I could've been dead. I could've died – '

His assistant slapped him. 'Keep it together, man.' Then he whistled. 'Hey, we got a dead door over here!'

Two geeky monsters came running

forward. 'Look out! Out of the way! Coming through!' they called. The geeks taped a yellow X on the door. Then they loaded the door into a shredder. With a loud grinding noise, the shredder chewed up the door, spewing wood chips out at the other end. When kids weren't scareable any more, their doors had to be destroyed.

The floor manager watched and shook his head. 'We've lost fifty-eight doors this week, sir,' he told his boss.

Waternoose sighed. 'Kids these days – they just don't get scared like they used to.'

At that moment, a child's scream came from behind a door, and Randall emerged. Suddenly the scoreboard switched. Randall's name replaced JAMES P. SULLIVAN in the number one spot. Sulley's name dropped to number two.

'Attention. We have a new scare leader: Randall Boggs,' Celia announced over the loudspeaker. A group of monsters swarmed around Randall, slapping him on the back and congratulating him.

Just then a little girl's scream escaped through Sulley's door, followed by another, then another and another! Mike could hardly replace the scream canisters fast enough to collect them all.

In a moment, Sulley came out of the door and cracked his knuckles. 'Slumber party,' he explained.

The scoreboard switched again. Sulley was back in the lead.

'Never mind,' announced Celia. The monsters crowding around Randall immediately ran over to Sulley. They slapped him on the back and cheered.

'Well, James, that was an impressive display,' Mr Waternoose said, scuttling over to Sulley.

'Oh, just doing my job, Mr Waternoose. Of course, I did learn from the best,' Sulley said modestly.

Waternoose chuckled and patted his hardworking employee on the back. Sulley had learned his scare moves from Waternoose himself. The older monster was proud of his Number One Scarer.

Randall watched them and growled with jealousy.

An assistant in the workstation next to Mike watched the scoreboard, impressed. 'Hey, Wazowski, nice job,' he said. 'Those numbers are pretty sweet.'

'Are they? I hadn't even noticed,' Mike answered, trying not to show his pride. 'And how's Georgie doing?'

'He's doing great. I love working with that big guy,' the assistant answered.

Just then George, a huge, hairy monster with a goofy grin, emerged from his door, doing a little tap dance. 'Keep the doors coming, Charlie. I'm on a roll today,' he told his assistant cheerfully. As he turned around, Mike and Charlie saw that a colourful little sock was stuck to his back.

Charlie's eyes opened wide with horror. 'Twenty-three nineteen! We have a twenty-three nineteen!' he shouted, pointing to the sock.

The panicked floor manager slammed his fist down on a button marked EMERGENCY. A siren wailed.

All the monsters on the Scare Floor turned to stare at George. 'George Sanderson, please remain motionless. Prepare for decontamination,' said the computerized voice.

'Get it off! Get it off!' George cried, frantically trying to brush the sock off his back.

Helicopters swarmed over the factory. Huge trucks from the Child Detection Agency (CDA) raced up to the building and screeched to a stop. A team of CDA agents dressed in protective gear jumped out. They shoved their way through the crowd of monsters.

'Please clear the contaminated area!' they shouted.

The CDA agents tackled poor George and knocked him to the ground. One agent lifted the sock off his back with a pair of tongs and placed it on the floor.

Another team of agents moved in. They set up a bomb on top of the sock, then quickly moved away.

Sulley covered his eyes. Mike covered his eye.

BOOM! In a blinding flash, the sock blew up. A CDA agent hurried forward and vacuumed up the dust to make sure not a trace of it remained.

George sighed with relief. 'Hey, thanks, guys. That was a close one,' he said.

But they weren't done yet! Suddenly a shower curtain sprang up around George and one of the agents. Another CDA agent handed a scary-looking electric razor to the agent inside the curtain.

'Aaaaaahh!' George screamed as the agent shaved him. Fur flew in every direction.

The shower went on and disinfectant rained down on George. *'Aaaaaaah!'* George screamed again. The shower curtain flew open. Out stepped a skinny, pimply, furless George. He looked more like a plucked chicken than a scary monster. A bandage covered the spot where the sock had been.

An agent reached out with a gloved hand and ripped the bandage off George's back. The big monster gulped with pain.

'OK, people!' the floor manager shouted. 'Take a break! We gotta shut down for a half hour and reset the system.'

Waternoose frowned. Shutting down the floor meant losing valuable scream-collecting time. 'What else can go wrong?' he said sadly. Sulley watched with concern as Waternoose sighed and slowly scuttled out of the room.

CHAPTER 5

The sun was setting over the city of Monstropolis. Inside the Monsters, Inc. factory, tired Scarers emerged from their last doors of the day. A large revolving rack returned the doors to the vault where they were kept.

'All doors must be returned,' the manager reminded everyone. 'No exceptions.'

Mike whistled as he looked over the paperwork for Sulley's scares. '*Whew* – you were on a roll, my man!' he told his friend.

Sulley nodded, pleased that he'd done

such good work. 'Another day like this and that scare record's in the bag.'

At five o'clock, Mike and Sulley were ready to go. Mike hurried through the lobby, eager to meet Celia for their date. But just as he reached her desk, Roz blocked his path.

'Hello, Wazowski,' Roz said, peering at him through her cat's-eye glasses. 'Fun-filled evening planned for tonight?'

'Well, as a matter of fact – ' Mike started.

But Roz cut him off. 'I'm sure you filed your paperwork correctly – for once.'

'*Eep!*' Mike exclaimed. He'd forgotten to file his scare reports! In fact, he hadn't filed his scare reports in weeks. Mike knew he was in big trouble with Roz. But he also knew that if he and Celia didn't get to the restaurant in five minutes, they'd lose their reservation! 'Oh, no!' he cried. 'What am I going to tell – '

Suddenly Celia came up behind Mike.

'Schmoopsie-Poo!' Mike said, panicked.

'Hey, Googly Bear! Want to get going?' Celia asked.

Mike was tongue-tied. He knew Celia would be angry if he cancelled their plans. 'Oh, do I ever ... It's just that ... uh ...'

'It's just that I forgot about some paperwork,' Sulley said, quickly coming to Mike's rescue. He could file the reports for Mike. 'Mike was reminding me. Thanks, buddy!'

'I was? I mean, I *was*!' Mike said, relieved. 'They're on my desk,' he told Sulley as he and Celia headed out the door.

Sulley returned to the Scare Floor and went to Mike's desk. He picked up a stack of paperwork.

Turning around, Sulley noticed a lone door in a workstation.

He looked around. Whose was it? All the doors should have been returned to the door vault. Just then Sulley realized that the red light above the door was on, which meant someone was using it.

Sulley opened the door and stuck his head inside. 'Hello? Hey, is anybody scaring in here?' he asked in a loud whisper.

Hearing no answer, Sulley shut the door. He tapped the blinking red light – maybe there was something wrong with it.

Suddenly Sulley heard a sound behind him *Thump*. What was that? Sulley paused. He heard the sound again. *Thump*. Sulley spun around and saw – a little girl!

The tiny, pigtailed tot looked up at Sulley with big brown eyes. Then she smiled and grabbed his tail.

'Aaaaaaah!' Sulley screamed. Looking frantically around, he spied a pair of tongs. He grabbed them and used them to pick up the girl. Holding the toxic toddler at arm's length, Sulley rushed over to her door, opened it, and placed

her inside. He closed the door and spun around – only to find her on the Scare Floor again!

The little girl giggled. 'Ayha!' she cried.

'*Aaaaaaah!*' Sulley screamed again. This time he grabbed the little girl with his bare hands, carried her all the way into the bedroom, and dropped her on the bed. As he ran towards the door, he got caught in a mobile hanging from the ceiling. Then he accidentally stepped in a laundry basket and fell down. The fall sent Sulley flying out of the door. He landed on the Scare Floor, covered with human kid things!

Just then Sulley heard a creaking noise in the hallway. Someone was coming! Quickly he sprinted into the Scarers' locker room. And not a moment too soon. Seconds later Randall wheeled a cart up to the door and entered the little girl's bedroom.

In the locker-room, Sulley began frantically stuffing the child's clothes and toys into a toilet. He didn't want to get caught with a bunch of kid things on him! But when he flushed the toilet, it overflowed. Everything spilled out on to the floor.

Scooping the soggy stuff up again, Sulley ran to the lockers. He opened a random locker, threw everything inside, and slammed the door shut. It was over. Breathing a sigh of relief, Sulley began to make his way out of the locker-room.

But only seconds later, he was back, screaming at the top of his lungs. The little girl was clinging to his back! He managed to shake her off as he ran to a corner of the room. The giant blue monster climbed on top of a bench and stood there, shivering with fear. The little girl peered up at him. 'Kitty!' she said.

'Oh, no! Stay back!' Sulley cried.

The girl giggled and babbled. She picked up a Monsters, Inc. hard hat and tried it on. Sulley saw his chance. When she wasn't looking, the monster scooped her into a large duffel bag.

He dashed back to the Scare Floor. But just as he was about to open the little girl's door and toss her back inside, the doorknob jiggled. Someone was coming out! Sulley was trapped!

Sulley moved to the other side of the door as it opened and Randall stepped out. He pushed a button, sending the door back to storage. The door rose into the air, exposing Sulley and his kid cargo. But Randall didn't see them. He had already turned to go.

Suddenly Randall stopped. Did he hear something? Sulley held his breath. But just as the little girl made a noise, Randall sneezed, covering up the sound.

Whew! That was a close one! Sulley watched Randall leave. Then he picked up the duffel bag and dashed out of the Monsters, Inc. building.

CHAPTER 6

Whack! A monster sushi chef chopped the head off a raw monster fish, then sliced it into a delicious monster meal. A dapper waiter picked up the sushi and whisked it off to a customer.

Mike and Celia sat in a booth in the fancy restaurant. They had just finished dinner. Snuggled together, the two lovebirds gazed into each other's eye.

'Oh, Michael,' Celia said with a sigh. 'I've had a lot of birthda –' She changed her mind and stopped. 'Well, not a *lot* of birthdays... but this is the best birthday ever.'

'You know, I was just thinking about the first time I laid eye on you – how pretty you looked,' Mike told Celia.

She and her snakes blushed. 'Stop it!' she cried teasingly.

'Your hair was shorter then.'

Celia nodded. 'I'm thinking about getting it cut.' The snakes on Celia's head looked up, panic-stricken. *Cut?*

'No, no,' Mike said. 'I like it this length.' The snakes sighed with relief.

'I like everything about you,' Mike went on. 'Just the other day, someone asked me who I thought was the most beautiful monster in all of Monstropolis. Do you know what I said?'

'What did you say?' Celia asked, batting her eyelashes.

'I said – ' Mike suddenly looked up in surprise. 'Sulley?' Behind Celia, Sulley was pressing his big blue face against the restaurant window, peering in.

'Sulley!' Celia exclaimed.

'No, no, no! That's not what I was

going to say! I mean, well, sure he's handsome...if you like the big, rugged, hairy...' Mike babbled. Had he really just seen Sulley? He looked at the window again, but Sulley was gone.

Celia was confused. 'Mike, you're not making sense – ' she began.

Suddenly Sulley appeared at the table. He was carrying a large duffel bag.

'Hi, guys!' he said nervously. 'What a coincidence, running into you here.' He squeezed into the booth, shoving up against Mike.

'Oof!' Celia grunted as Mike knocked into her. The couple looked at Sulley in surprise.

'Sulley,' Mike growled through gritted teeth.

'Uh, I'm just going to order a takeaway,' Sulley said. He grabbed a menu and held it up like a screen, blocking himself and Mike from Celia's view. 'I wonder what's good here.'

Behind the menu, Mike glared at

Sulley. 'Get out of here. You're ruining everything!' he whispered angrily.

'I went back to get your paperwork, and there was a door,' Sulley whispered.

'What?' Mike stopped to consider this. He peeked out from behind the menu, grinned at the furious Celia, and ducked back down. 'A door?' he asked, confused.

Sulley nodded. 'Randall was in it.'

'Wait a minute. Randall?' Suddenly it dawned on Mike. 'That cheater! He's trying to boost his scare numbers!'

Sulley looked worried. 'There's something else . . .'

'What?' Mike asked.

'Look in the bag.' Sulley motioned towards the duffel bag under the table.

Mike ducked under the table. A second later, he popped back up. 'What bag?'

Sulley looked down, panicked. The bag was gone!

At that moment, a scream arose from a monster couple posing for a photo. As they were smiling for the camera, the little girl had popped up on the photographer's shoulder. The girl turned and hung upside down in front of the photographer's face.

'*Ahhhhhh!* A kid!' the photographer yelled in terror. His camera flashed as the little girl bounced off him.

'Boo!' she said. The monster diners screamed and scrambled out of her way.

A sushi chef grabbed a phone and dialled an emergency number. 'There's a kid here!' he shouted into the receiver. 'A human kid!'

Panicked monsters ran this way and that. Sulley stumbled around, trying to catch the little girl, but she dodged out of the way. In the confusion, Mike ran headfirst into a pile of cardboard take-away boxes.

Grabbing one, Mike nervously scooped the girl inside, being careful not to touch a single hair on her toxic little head. With one quick motion, Sulley shut the lid of the box.

'Come on!' Sulley cried.

Gripping the box, Mike and Sulley headed for the door. Just as they got outside, vans and helicopters from the Child Detection Agency arrived. CDA agents charged into the restaurant.

'Stand clear, please,' they commanded, pushing through the crowd.

In all the commotion, Celia had been separated from Mike. 'Michael! Michael!' she called, chasing after him.

Mike spun around. 'Oh, Celia!' he said. He'd almost forgotten about his date!

But a CDA agent blocked Celia's path. 'Come with us, please,' he said, herding her to one side.

'Stop pushing!' Celia snapped.

'Hey!' Mike shouted at the agent. 'Get your hands off my Schmoopsie-Poo!'

But Sulley grabbed him. This was no time for romance! The two dashed off just as a CDA agent announced,

'Number One gives the OK for decon.' A crew of agents scurried forward to set up the decontamination bombs.

Mike and Sulley sprinted down an alley. 'Well,' Mike said, panting, 'I don't think that date could have gone any worse!'

Just then – *BOOM!* – the restaurant exploded behind them.

CHAPTER 7

Later, in their apartment, Sulley and Mike watched the explosion again on the evening news.

'If witnesses are to be believed, there has been a child security breach for the first time in monster history,' the newsreader grimly announced.

The TV glowed with images of the smouldering sushi restaurant after the decontamination. A reporter interviewed one of the CDA agents. 'We can neither confirm nor deny the presence of a human child here tonight,' the agent said.

Another monster being interviewed

said, 'Well, a kid flew right over me and blasted a car with its laser vision!'

'I tried to run from it, but it picked me up with its mind powers and shook me like a doll!' reported yet another monster.

A monster with many eyes stepped up to the camera. 'It's t-true!' he stammered. 'I saw the whole thing!'

The TV report returned to the newsreader, who was in the studio interviewing cultural studies professor Dr Frasenburger about the recent events. 'It is my professional opinion that now is the time to panic!' Dr Frasenburger said, leaping up from the desk and panicking.

But before Sulley and Mike heard what else Dr Frasenburger had to say, the TV set suddenly tipped forward. It fell on to the floor with a crash. A little girl's familiar head peeked over the toppled set.

'Uh-oh,' she said.

'Aaaaah!' Mike and Sulley screamed.

They jumped behind a chair. The little girl began to walk towards the terrified monsters.

'It's coming! It's coming!' Mike cried fearfully. His voice was muffled by the snorkel tube that he was using to breathe through. Mike wasn't taking any chances with kid germs. He'd placed a metal strainer over his eye and armed himself with a giant can of disinfectant spray.

Sulley and Mike scrambled over to the window. Outside, helicopters circled Monstropolis, searching for the dangerous child. Mike yanked down the blind. They certainly didn't want anyone to find out the kid was in *their* apartment.

Just then the girl popped up from behind a chair and ran towards them, babbling happily.

The monsters dodged out of the way. The girl reached up and tugged at the window blind, which flapped open. Peering out of the window, the little girl waved at the helicopters.

Randall brags to Sulley and Mike about
his scaring abilities.

Sulley is the Number One Scarer at Monsters, Inc.

Uh-oh! A human child is in the factory!

Kitty!

The kid likes Sulley.

Oh no! Sulley is tangled up in the kid's toys!

**Sulley is afraid of the kid, because
he thinks she's toxic.**

Mike and Celia are on a date.

The monsters try to entertain the little girl to keep her quiet.

Mike has a plan, but it's not a very good one.

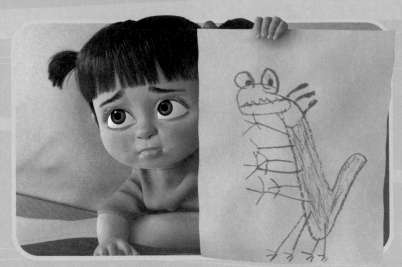

Boo shows Sulley a picture of
Randall, her Scarer.

Sulley tries to convince Mike that
Boo is not toxic.

Boo, disguised as a baby monster, plays hide-and-seek with Sulley.

Mike tries to put Boo back through the first door he can find.

Randall wants to find Boo in order to
carry out his secret plan.

The monsters finally find Boo's closet door.

Mike grabbed a broom and used it to lift the child away from the window. As soon as he'd moved her, Mike quickly sprayed disinfectant on the spot where she'd been standing. But no sooner had the girl jumped off the broom than she discovered Mike's CD collection. The CDs were arranged in neat little piles. The girl reached towards them.

'No!' Mike cried. 'Don't touch those, you little – '

The girl pulled a single CD from the middle of a tall pile. The entire stack collapsed.

'Oh!' Mike moaned. 'Those were alphabetized . . .' Mike lifted the strainer from his eye. 'It's all right,' he reassured himself. 'As long as it doesn't come near us, we're gonna be OK.'

Just then the little girl popped up next to Mike and sneezed on his arm.

Mike screamed and began to wildly spray disinfectant at the spot where she'd sneezed. Unfortunately he had the can turned the wrong way. The spray hit him right in the eye. *'Ahhh!'* He screamed in pain.

Meanwhile, the girl was creeping towards Sulley. He moved backwards until he was pressed up against a chair next to the fireplace. Suddenly the child babbled and pointed to a teddy bear sitting on the mantelpiece.

Sulley grabbed the teddy bear. 'Oh, here – you like this?' he asked. 'Fetch.' He threw the teddy bear over the child's head. She chased it.

Mike, whose eye was bright red from the disinfectant, gasped when he saw the girl holding his bear. 'That's it!' he declared. He ran over and swiped the bear out of the little girl's hands. 'No one touches little Mikey!'

The girl whimpered. Her eyes filled with tears.

'Mike, give her the bear,' Sulley said in a cautious tone. But Mike held tight. The girl opened her mouth and . . .

screamed!

Mike and Sulley covered their ears. Suddenly the lights in the apartment flared up.

Outside, the circling helicopters turned and began to fly in the direction of their apartment.

Panicking, Mike dropped the teddy bear and ran to shut the window blind again. 'Make it stop, Sulley!' he cried, peeking out of the window.

Sulley picked up the bear and offered it to the girl. 'Here, see the bear? Nice bear.'

But it was no use. She cried even harder. The lights continued to blaze. Desperately Sulley began to sing a song and make the bear dance.

'Keep it up! You're doing great!' Mike said. Slowly the girl stopped crying. The lights in the apartment returned to normal. The helicopters began to fly away. Sulley and Mike breathed a sigh of relief.

But Sulley was still holding the bear, and

now the little girl wanted it. She reached out, but it was high up in Sulley's big hand. Frustrated, she began to cry again.

'Sulley, the bear! Give it the – ' Mike ran forward. Just then he hit a slick spot on the floor. *'Whooooahh!'* Mike flew into the air and landed in a rubbish bin.

The little girl let out a big belly laugh. Suddenly all the lights in the entire apartment building surged even brighter than before. Then they burned out!

'What was that?' Sulley asked when the girl stopped laughing.

'I have no idea, but it would be really great if it didn't do it again,' Mike replied. At this rate, the CDA would find them in no time. The little girl started to giggle again.

'Shhhh,' Sulley said to the girl, putting a furry finger to his lips.

Amazingly, the child seemed to understand. She held a tiny finger up to her own mouth. 'Shhhh,' she said. She grinned at Sulley.

CHAPTER 8

A little while later, the girl was sitting on the living-room floor, happily drawing pictures and munching pieces of cereal that Sulley tossed to her from across the room.

Sulley, however, was not as happy. He sat in a chair with his head in his hands. 'How could I be so stupid?' he asked. 'This could destroy the company.'

'Who cares about the company? What about us?' said Mike. 'That thing is a killing machine!' He pointed to the tiny girl, who was now spinning in circles, shaking her pigtails from side to side.

'La la la la la,' she sang.

Mike shuddered. 'I bet it's just waiting for us to fall asleep and then ... *Wham!* We're easy prey, my friend. We're sitting targets.'

'*Uh,*' the toddler grunted, falling down on her bottom.

Suddenly Mike snapped his fingers. He knew how to get them out of this mess! 'OK, look, I think I have a plan here,' he told Sulley. He took a piece of paper and began to draw. 'Using mainly spoons, we dig a tunnel under the city and then release it into the wild.'

Sulley looked at him. 'Spoons,' he said in disbelief.

Mike crumpled the paper and tossed it on to a pile of wadded-up plans. He put his head down on the desk. 'That's it. I'm out of ideas. Hot-air balloons – too expensive. Giant slingshot – too conspicuous. Enormous wooden horse – too Greek!' He sighed.

Sulley looked down at the girl. She

held up a drawing she'd made of herself and the big blue monster. Then she put her crayon down and yawned.

'Uh, Mike, I think she's getting tired,' Sulley said.

'Well, then why don't you find a place for it to sleep while I think of a plan?' Mike snapped.

Using pieces of cereal, Sulley led the girl into his bedroom. She followed him, picking up the cereal and popping it into her mouth with one hand. In the other hand she carried one of her drawings.

Sulley spread sheets of newspaper on the floor and poured a small pile of cereal on them. 'OK,' he told the child. 'I'm making a nice little area for you to – '

The girl giggled. Sulley turned around and saw that she'd climbed on to his bed.

Sulley ran to stop her. 'Hey, that's *my* bed. You're gonna get your germs all over it.' But the girl wasn't moving. 'Ah, fine.' Sulley sighed. 'My chair's more comfortable anyway.' He started to leave the room.

But before he could go, the little girl cried out and pointed nervously at the closet.

'It's just a closet,' Sulley told her. 'Will you go to sleep?' The girl held up the drawing she'd made. Sulley looked at the paper.

'Hey, that looks like Randall,' he said. Suddenly he realized that it was a picture of Randall. He must be the girl's assigned monster! She thought Randall was going to come out of the closet and scare her.

'Oh, boy,' said Sulley. 'How do I explain this?' Sulley crossed over to the closet and opened the door. The little girl squealed and pulled the covers over her head.

'No monster in here,' Sulley told her confidently. He stepped inside the closet. 'Well, *now* there is. But *I'm* not gonna scare you. I'm off duty.'

The girl peered into the closet. She wasn't quite convinced.

'OK, how 'bout I sit here until you fall asleep?' Sulley suggested, pulling a breeze block up in front of the closet. He put his hands together and pretended they were a pillow. 'Go ahead, go to sleep.' He made some snoring noises to encourage her.

The girl giggled. Seconds later, she was fast asleep.

Sulley heaved a sigh of relief. He looked at the little girl. She was actually quite sweet, he thought. He returned to the living-room. 'Hey, Mike. This might sound crazy, but I don't think that kid's dangerous,' he said.

'Really?' Mike answered. 'Well, in that case, let's keep it. I always wanted a pet . . . *that could kill me*!'

'Look,' Sulley said calmly, 'what if we just put her back in her door?'

'What?' Mike said. He looked at Sulley as if he'd lost his mind.

'Think about it,' Sulley said. 'If we send her back, it's like it never happened. Everything goes back to normal.'

'Tell me you're joking,' Mike said. Sulley shook his head. Mike stared at his friend. Sulley *had* lost his mind. 'That is a *horrible* idea!' Mike exclaimed. 'What are we gonna do, march right out into public with that thing? *Then* I guess we just waltz right up to the factory, right?'

Sulley nodded, lost in thought. He was already coming up with his own plan.

CHAPTER 9

First thing the next morning, Mike, Sulley and the kid were marching through a crowded Monstropolis street. They'd disguised the girl in a purple monster costume made from the upholstery on Sulley's living-room chair. Sulley carried the little 'monster' behind his back.

'I can't believe we are waltzing right up to the factory!' Mike exclaimed as they walked along. He yanked the child's hood down lower on her head. 'Sulley,' he begged his friend, 'a mop, a couple of lights, and some chair fabric are not gonna fool anyone. Just think about a few names:

Loch Ness, Bigfoot, the Abominable Snowman. They've all got one thing in common, pal – banishment! We could be next!' Even more than he feared kids, Mike feared being sent off to live in the human world.

'Don't panic. We can do this,' Sulley told him as they reached the Monsters, Inc. building.

But inside the lobby, the two friends were in for a surprise – the place was crawling with CDA agents! The head agent was talking to Mr Waternoose. As Mike and Sulley watched, he held up the charred remains of the duffel bag that Sulley had used to carry the girl into the restaurant. The Monsters, Inc. logo was printed on the side.

'This was recovered at the scene,' the agent informed Waternoose.

'Don't panic. Don't panic!' Sulley said through clenched teeth.

'Don't tell me not to panic!' Mike said out the side of his mouth.

'Boo!' said the little girl. Somehow she'd gotten away – and she was headed straight for Waternoose! She tugged on one of his large crab legs.

'Oh! Hello, little one!' Waternoose said, looking down and patting her on the head. 'Where did you come from?' The costume worked! He thought she was a little monster!

Sulley and Mike rushed over to him. Waternoose looked up at them. As he did, the hood of the girl's costume fell off. Her face was showing! Mike and Sulley gulped.

But Waternoose didn't notice. 'James!' he said to Sulley. 'Why don't you stop by the simulator after lunch today and give us a scare demonstration?' He wanted Sulley to show some new scare recruits what it took to be a top Scarer.

'Oh, sir, uh, today might be a little – ' Sulley started. But before he could finish, Waternoose was distracted by the CDA agent.

'I'll see you this afternoon, James,' Waternoose said, turning away.

'Great,' Mike said sarcastically.

Sulley picked up the girl, and the three started to leave. Just then a CDA agent passed them. His kid detector buzzed loudly.

'Halt!' the agent cried. He grabbed an innocent monster who happened to be passing at the same time. While the agent was distracted, Mike and Sulley beat a hasty retreat to the locker-room.

'Come on! The coast is clear!' Mike whispered, peering around a row of lockers. Nervously the trio moved into the locker-room.

'Wait here while I get its card key,' Mike said in a low voice. He turned to head out of the door.

'But she can't stay here,' Sulley said. 'This is the *men's* room.'

Mike stopped and looked at his friend. 'That is the weirdest thing you have ever said,' he told Sulley. 'It's fine! Look, it loves it here! It's dancing with joy!'

Sulley looked at the little girl in the monster costume. She was indeed doing a little dance.

'I'll be right back with its door key,' Mike said.

As Mike left, the little girl kept dancing, holding the flippers of her costume close to her body.

Sulley chuckled. 'That's a cute little dance. It almost looks like you've got to – '

The hood of her costume fell back. The little girl's face was scrunched up. Suddenly Sulley understood – she had to go to the toilet.

'Oh,' he said.

While Sulley waited, the girl hummed cheerfully inside a cubicle. Finally the humming stopped. Sulley heard a flush. He waited for a moment, but she didn't come out.

'You're finished, right?' Sulley called. He opened the door. But no one was in the cubicle!

Sulley rushed to the toilet and looked at the water swirling down the drain. Had she fallen in? Just as he was about to jam his arm into the toilet bowl, he heard a laugh behind him. Sulley spun around.

'Boo!' said the little girl. *Whew!* Sulley sighed with relief. She grinned and giggled. Then she took off down the row of cubicles. She wanted to play hide-and-seek!

Sulley watched as the child hid in a cubicle. 'Where did she go?' Sulley said loudly, playing along. 'Did she disappear? Did she turn invisible? I just have no idea.' He crossed over to where she'd hidden. 'Gotcha!' he said, opening the door. But the cubicle was empty.

The little girl peeked out from a cubicle two doors down. 'Hey!' Sulley said. 'You're good!'

Meanwhile, Mike was trying to charm Roz into giving him the card key for the little girl's door. 'Roz, my tender oozing blossom,' he said, leaning into her workstation. 'You're looking fabulous today. Is that a new haircut?'

Roz looked back at him, expressionless.

'Come on, tell me. That's got to be a new haircut. New makeup? You've had a lift? You've had a tuck? You've had something?'

Roz continued to stare at him.

'Listen,' Mike said at last, 'I need a favour. Randall was working late last night out on the Scare Floor. I *really* need the key for the door he was using.'

'Well, isn't that nice,' Roz said. 'But guess what? You didn't turn in your paperwork last night.'

'He didn't? You mean, I didn't?' Mike said in surprise.

'This office is now closed,' Roz said. She slammed the front panel of her desk shut – right on Mike's fingers.

'Aaahhh!' He squealed in pain.

Mike returned to the locker-room

empty-handed, only to find Sulley crawling around the floor on his hands and knees.

'Ready or not, here I come!' the big monster said, peering under the cubicle.

'What are you doing?' Mike asked.

Sulley jumped to his feet. 'Uh, I'm looking for the kid.'

'You lost it?' Mike cried.

'No, she was just . . . ' Sulley started to explain. Just then the little girl ran up and clung to Sulley's arm. 'Here she is,' Sulley said, lifting the arm with the kid attached.

The girl whimpered. 'What's the matter?' Sulley asked. But then he realized Randall had just entered the locker-room! In a flash, the three ran into a cubicle and shut the door. A second later, Randall came into the room.

Fungus was right behind him. 'Randall, what are we going to do about the child?' he asked in a worried whisper.

'Shhh!' Randall said, grabbing Fungus's chin and clamping his mouth shut. He looked around the locker-room. Suddenly he disappeared!

Slam! The door to a cubicle banged open. *Slam!* The next door opened. Randall was kicking in the doors to each of the cubicles! Sulley, Mike and the little girl crouched on the toilet in their cubicle, holding their breath.

But just as Randall was about to kick in their door, Fungus popped up in front of him. He held up a newspaper. 'It's on the front page!' he exclaimed. 'I did a simple calculation, factoring in the size of the sushi restaurant. The child may have survived!'

'Well, until we know for sure, we're gonna act like nothing happened,' Randall told Fungus. 'You just get the machine up and running. I'll take care of the kid. And when I find whoever let it out . . . they're dead!'

CHAPTER 10

'They're gone,' Sulley whispered as soon as Fungus and Randall left the room. Suddenly there was a splash. Mike had fallen into the toilet.

'*Ewww,*' said the little girl.

But Mike wasn't thinking about his wet feet. He was thinking about what Randall had said. 'This is bad. This is so very bad,' he muttered as the trio hurried down the hall back to the Scare Floor.

'What were they talking about? A machine?' Sulley wondered.

'Who cares?' Mike answered him frantically.

'Look, don't panic,' Sulley told him. 'All we have to do is call her door down and send her home.'

When they reached the Scare Floor, Mike and Sulley whistled casually, trying to attract as little attention as possible. 'You got her card key, right?' Sulley asked Mike out the corner of his mouth.

'Of course I have her card key,' Mike lied. As they walked past a group of assistants, he reached out and stole a key from one of their folders.

At their workstation, Mike slid the card into the slot. The rack above the Scare Floor powered up. Sulley and Mike waited nervously for the door to slide into position.

'Take care of yourself. And try not to run through any more closets,' Sulley whispered to the little girl.

A door landed in the station. Sulley blinked. 'Mike, that's not her door,' he said.

'Of course it's her door!' Mike said.

He opened it. Yodelling came piping out.

'No,' Sulley said. 'Her door was white. And it had flowers on it.'

But Mike wasn't listening. He was determined to send the girl through the door – any door. He leaned down to say good-bye to the kid, careful not to get too close. 'OK, send me a postcard, kid. That's *Miiike* Wa*zowww*ski.'

'Mike Wazowski!' the girl exclaimed.

'Very good,' Mike said. He threw a pencil through the door. 'Go get the stick. Go fetch,' he told her.

Just then a big blue hand reached out and closed the door. 'Mike, this isn't Boo's door,' Sulley said sternly.

' "Boo"? What's "Boo"?' Mike asked.

'That's what I decided to call her,' Sulley said. 'Is there a problem?'

'Sulley, you're not supposed to name it!' Mike said, his voice rising. He began to shout. *'Now put that thing back where it came from, or so help me . . .'*

Suddenly Mike shut his mouth.

A number of assistants and CDA agents had turned to look at them.

'Oh, hey, we're rehearsing a scene for the upcoming company play called . . . uh, *Put That Thing Back Where It Came From . . . Or So Help Me!*' Mike said, covering up quickly. He started to sing. 'Put that thing back where it came from, or so help me . . .' Sulley hummed along.

The other monsters went back to their work. But when Sulley and Mike turned around, Boo was gone!

Mike suddenly cheered up. 'Wait a minute! This is perfect! She's gone!' He tried to hold Sulley back. 'Somebody else will find the kid! It'll be their problem – not ours. She's out of our hair!'

But Sulley wasn't going to lose Boo. With Mike clinging to his tail, Sulley ran through the halls in search of his little human friend. Rounding a corner, he slammed right into Randall!

'What are you two doing?' Randall

asked suspiciously.

'They're rehearsing a play,' said a passing assistant.

'She's out of our hair...' sang Mike, trying desperately to cover up once again.

Randall ignored him. 'Word on the street is the kid's been traced back to this factory. You haven't seen anything, have you?' he said with a snarl.

'Well ... uh ... no,' Sulley stammered nervously. Boo, still disguised as a monster, began to waddle down the hall. Sulley edged away from Randall and followed her.

'No way!' said Mike. 'But if it was an inside job, I – I'd put my money on Waxford. You know, he's got them shifty eyes.' Mike pointed his thumb towards a monster with several shifty eyes.

'Hey, Waxford ...' Randall's eyes narrowed as he moved off to question the monster.

Mike breathed a sigh of relief and turned around – to find himself face to face with a furious Celia! She was wearing a brace around her neck. Her snakes all had little braces around their necks, too.

'Michael Wazowski! Last night was one of the worst nights of my entire life!' she yelled. Her snakes hissed angrily at Mike.

Mike's eye nearly bugged out of his head. He glanced over at Randall. 'Shhh! Honey, I thought you liked sushi,' he whispered.

'Sushi!' Celia roared. 'You think this is about *sushi*?'

Randall stopped in his tracks. Mike saw him. Desperate to keep Celia quiet, he grabbed her and planted a huge kiss on her lips.

But Randall had heard enough. He held up the newspaper Fungus had given him. There, right on the front page, was a picture of Mike.

'Wazowski!' Randall hissed. He spun around – but Mike was already gone!

CHAPTER 11

Panicked, Mike tore down the halls of Monsters, Inc. As he stopped to catch his breath, Randall unblended from the wall right next to him.

'Yikes!' Mike shrieked.

Randall grabbed Mike and pushed him against the wall. 'Where's the kid?' he growled.

'You're not pinning this on me!' Mike replied. 'It never would have gotten out if you hadn't been cheating last night!'

Randall smiled evilly. So Mike thought that was what this was all about. 'Cheating. Right. OK, I think I know how to make this all go away. In five minutes everyone goes to lunch; the Scare Floor will be empty. You see that clock?' He grabbed Mike's arms to emphasize his point. 'When the big hand is pointing up and the little hand is pointing up, the kid's door will be in my station.' He yanked Mike's arms into the twelve o'clock position. 'But when the big hand points down . . .' He twisted Mike's arm. Mike winced. '. . . The door will be gone. You have until then to put the kid back.' Randall gave Mike's arm one last twist, then disappeared.

Meanwhile, Sulley was chasing Boo. He'd almost caught up with her when suddenly she fell into a rubbish bin! Before he could reach her, two geeky monsters dumped the rubbish into a rubbish compressor. Sulley hurried to the rubbish room, but it was too late. He picked up a cube of compressed rubbish. One of the monster eyeballs from Boo's costume poked out.

When Mike found him, Sulley was cradling the rubbish cube and crying. 'I can still hear her little voice,' Sulley sobbed.

'Mike Wazowski!' said a little girl's voice.

'Hey,' Mike said, putting his ear near the cube. 'I can hear her, too.'

'Mike Wazowski!' said several little voices.

'How many kids you got in there?' Mike asked, staring at the cube.

Sulley whipped around. There was Boo, minus one monster eyeball from her costume, toddling along with a day-care class of little monsters. She hadn't been compacted after all! Sulley ran over and scooped her up.

'Don't you ever run away from me again, young lady!' he said, hugging her tightly.

'OK, Sulley. That's enough. Let's go,' Mike said through clenched teeth. Just then one of the little monster kids sank its teeth into Mike's arm. Mike yelped in pain, and Boo started laughing.

The lights overhead glowed brightly. Light-bulbs began to pop. The day-care class screamed and ran away.

'Stop making Boo laugh!' Sulley told Mike as they hurried back to the Scare Floor.

When they arrived, they found Boo's door in its station. 'There it is! Just like Randall said!' Mike exclaimed with relief.

'Randall!' exclaimed Sulley, confused. Boo squirmed out of his arms and ran to hide under a desk. 'Mike, what are you thinking?' Sulley asked as he coaxed Boo out. 'We can't trust Randall! He's after Boo!'

'Look, Sulley. You wanted her door and there it is,' Mike said. 'Now let's move.'

'No, Mike,' Sulley said, holding Boo tightly.

'You want me to prove everything's on

the up-and-up?' Mike asked. 'Fine!' He marched over to Boo's door and walked inside. While Sulley and Boo watched, Mike started jumping on the bed. One jump. Two jumps. On the third jump, a large plastic box flew up from the bed and covered him. It was a trap!

CHAPTER 12

Sulley and Boo hid under a desk as Randall emerged through Boo's door, carrying the box with Mike inside. Looking over his shoulder, Randall loaded the box on to a cart and quickly wheeled it off the Scare Floor. Sulley grabbed Boo and followed him.

The lizard monster moved quickly. Sulley tried desperately to keep up with him, but the hallways were crowded with Monsters, Inc. employees returning from their lunch break. He lost sight of Randall. When Sulley turned a corner, he found himself at a dead end.

Sulley looked around, confused. Meanwhile, Boo began to play with some tools that hung on a panel on the wall. Suddenly the panel swung open, revealing a secret passageway!

'Boo, way to go!' Sulley cheered.

Carrying Boo, Sulley hurried down the dark corridor. At the end, he discovered a grimy, dimly lit laboratory. Randall and Fungus were inside. Hidden behind a wall of pipes, Sulley watched them.

'I got the kid!' Randall told Fungus. 'Get over here and help me! Come on – while we're still young.'

Randall and Fungus pulled the box off the cart and opened it to find – Mike!

'Wazowski!' Randall exclaimed, shocked. 'Where is it, you little one-eyed cretin?' he asked angrily.

'You're nuts if you think kidnapping me is gonna help you cheat your way to the top!' Mike told him.

Randall gave a sinister chuckle. 'You still think this is about that stupid scare record?'

'Well, I did right up until you chuckled like that,' Mike said weakly. 'And now I'm thinking I should just get out of here.'

But Randall wasn't about to let Mike go anywhere. 'I'm about to revolutionize the scaring industry,' he said. 'And when I do, even the great James P. Sullivan is gonna be working for me. First I need to know where the kid is – and you're going to tell me.'

A vacuum-like machine lowered from the ceiling. It began to move slowly towards Mike's face. 'Uh-oh. What is that thing?' Mike cried. The machine began to suck Mike's lips towards it.

Sulley looked around frantically for a way to save his friend. He spotted some wires leading to a power point. Reaching over, Sulley pulled the plug. The machine stopped with a whir.

'Go check the machine!' Randall snapped at Fungus. And then Randall noticed the wires moving on the floor. 'Hmmm,' he said suspiciously. He followed the wires to the wall, plugged them back in and returned to the machine.

But when he got there, his jaw dropped in surprise. Mike was gone and Fungus was strapped in his place! The vacuum-like machine was sucking the scream right out of Fungus!

Randall hit a switch and turned off the machine. 'Where is he?' Randall shouted furiously.

But Fungus couldn't speak. Lifting one weak arm, he pointed to the exit through which Mike, Sulley and Boo had escaped.

CHAPTER 13

The three friends raced out of the secret passageway and back into the Monsters, Inc. factory. But they weren't out of danger yet! At the end of the hallway, a group of CDA agents were still searching for clues.

'We gotta get out of here *now*!' Mike exclaimed. 'We can start a whole new life somewhere far away!' He ran towards a door marked EXIT. 'Good-bye, Monsters, Inc. Good-bye, Mr Waternoose!'

'Wait!' said Sulley. 'Follow me! I have an idea!' He turned and ran back the way they'd come.

'No, no, no, no!' Mike cried, running after Sulley.

'Simulation terminated. Simulation terminated,' said a computerized voice.

'No, no, no, no!' Waternoose was yelling at a roomful of monster recruits in the simulator room. 'What was that? You're trying to *scare* the kid – not lull it to sleep! How many times do I have to tell you? It's all about how you enter the room!'

At that moment Sulley burst into the room. Mike was right on his tail. 'Mr Waternoose!' Sulley cried.

'James! Perfect timing!' Waternoose declared. 'Now show these monsters how it's done.'

'No, sir, you don't understand . . .' Sulley protested. But Waternoose grabbed Boo out of Sulley's hands and passed her to Mike.

'Pay attention, everyone,' he told the recruits. 'You're about to see the best in the business!' The lights in the room dimmed. The puppet boy was reset in his place in the bed. Boo wiggled out of Mike's arms and ran to be near Sulley.

'Now give us a big, loud roar,' Waternoose told Sulley. Sulley paused. 'What are you waiting for?' Waternoose asked. 'Roar!'

Sulley sighed. He had no choice. Opening his mouth, he gave a mighty 'ROOOAAAARRR!'

The puppet kid screamed. Boo was terrified. Tears welled up in her eyes. As the monster recruits clapped, she ran to hide in the corner.

'Well done, James!' said Waternoose, ushering the recruits out of the room.

Sulley suddenly spotted Boo hiding in the shadows. 'Boo?' said Sulley gently. But she backed away from him, crying. Sulley no longer seemed like a cuddly friend to Boo. Now he seemed like a big scary monster!

As she tried to get away, Boo tripped.

The hood of her monster costume fell back.

Waternoose gasped. 'The child!'

Mike tried to explain. 'Sir, she isn't toxic. I know it sounds crazy, but trust me. Sulley and I have been with her since last night, and nothing's happened to us. We tried to get its door to send it back, but things didn't work out like we planned. It's not our fault – it's Randall's. He was trying to kidnap her. We thought he was just trying to cheat at first, but it's a lot bigger than cheating. He's got some kind of crazy torture machine that sucks the scream out of kids, and he was gonna test it out on that girl!'

'Randall!' Waternoose exclaimed.

Meanwhile, Sulley was still trying to reach Boo. But she ran away from him and hid behind one of Waternoose's legs. Waternoose scooped her up.

'Oh, I never thought things would come to this,' he said with a sigh. Holding Boo, he crossed to a door station and punched numbers into a keypad. 'I'm sorry you boys got mixed up in this . . . especially you, James. But now we can set everything straight again for the good of the company.' A huge metal door fell into the station.

'Uh, sir, that's not her door,' Sulley told him.

'I know,' Waternoose said. 'It's yours.'

Suddenly Randall unblended from the metal door. He opened it to reveal – falling snow! Sulley and Mike gasped.

With a mighty shove, Waternoose pushed the two monsters through the door and into the human world!

'Boo!' Sulley cried as he and Mike landed in a pile of snow. He looked up in time to see Waternoose slam the door shut. Sulley ran to the door. But when he opened it again, all he saw was falling snow. The opening to Monstropolis had closed.

'Oh, what a great idea, going to your old pal Waternoose,' Mike snapped.

'Too bad he was in on the whole thing!'

Sulley ignored him and tried the door again. The only thing he cared about was getting back to save Boo from Randall's machine. But the door stayed closed.

'All you had to do was listen to me,' Mike yelled, furious. He charged at Sulley. The two monsters rolled through the snow, fists flying.

Just then a huge shadow fell across them. The two looked up to see ... a giant, hairy monster! Mike and Sulley screamed!

CHAPTER 14

Shadows flickered on the wall of the Yeti's cavernous lair. The huge beast carried a tray of teacups to Mike and Sulley. Suddenly he grinned.

'Snow cone?' he asked, politely offering the tray of yellow snow cones to Mike. Mike looked at the treats, disgusted. 'Oh, no, don't worry – it's lemon,' the Yeti said, seeing Mike's reaction.

Mike didn't answer. He was huddled next to a lantern, trying to keep warm and glaring at Sulley. Sulley sat by the mouth of the cave, staring out at the snow. Snow drifted in and piled up on his fur.

'I understand,' the Yeti said. 'It ain't easy being banished. It won't be so hard for you guys – banished with your best friend.'

'He's not my friend!' Mike shouted. 'Ruined my life for a stupid kid!' he yelled at Sulley. 'Because of you, I'm stuck forever in this frozen wasteland!'

'Wasteland!' the Yeti said defensively. 'I think you mean *wonderland*. How about all this fabulous snow? And wait until you see the local village – cutest thing in the world – '

'What did you say?' Sulley said, interrupting. 'Something about a village? Where? Are there kids in it?' He ran across the cave and grabbed the Yeti.

'It's at the bottom of the mountain – take you at least three days,' the Yeti answered, a little scared by Sulley's enthusiasm.

Sulley growled. 'Three days!' That wasn't soon enough to save Boo! He punched the wall of the cave. A piece of ice split off and slid across the floor. All of a sudden Sulley got an idea!

He crossed the cave and began digging through the Yeti's collection of hiking gear. 'We need to get Boo,' Sulley announced.

A snowball flew across the room and hit Sulley in the face. He paused, then continued working on his project. Mike began to pack another snowball.

'Boo! What about us?' Mike said angrily. 'We were about to break the record! We would've had it made!'

'None of that matters now,' Sulley said, hammering away.

'None of it matters?' Mike shouted. 'What about everything we ever worked for? What about Celia? I'm never going to see her again! What about me? I'm your best friend. Do I matter?'

Sulley stopped working and turned to Mike. He'd built a sled! It had skis for runners and a ski pole for steering!

'I'm sorry, Mike. I'm sorry we're stuck

out here, but Boo's in trouble. I think there might be a way to save her, if we can just get – '

But Mike cut him off. 'We? If *you* want to go out there and freeze to death, be my guest. You're on your own.' He folded his arms and turned his back to Sulley.

Grabbing the lantern, Sulley took his sled out into the snow.

By the light of the swaying lantern, Sulley rocketed down the snowy mountainside. He whizzed between two huge rocks, narrowly missing them. The sled picked up speed. He was nearing the bottom!

Suddenly a giant boulder loomed up in his path. There was no way to turn! Sulley hit the boulder. One of the skis tore off the sled. Sulley went flying through the air and tumbled down the mountainside. At last he came to a stop. The big blue monster lay still in the snow.

It was all over. He would never reach Boo now.

But what was that sound? Sulley lifted his head and listened carefully. There it was again – the unmistakable sound of a child's scream. The fog lifted. In the distance, Sulley saw the village!

CHAPTER 15

George, the goofy monster who had been decontaminated the day before, walked cautiously up to his door station with a crutch. He was still pretty bruised from the CDA agents' decontamination.

'George, I know you can do this,' Charlie, his assistant, said encouragingly. 'I picked out an easy door for you in nice, quiet Nepal.'

'You're right,' George said. He handed Charlie his crutch and stepped up to the door.

At that moment, Sulley came running through the door, trampling poor George.

'Gangway! Look out! Coming through!' he yelled. 'Sorry, George,' he called over his shoulder as he dashed off.

Charlie's eyes opened wide. A child's sock was stuck to George's chest. He started to call out the contamination alert. 'Twenty-three –' But George wasn't going through *that* again! Before Charlie could finish, George grabbed his assistant, stuffed the sock into his mouth, and tossed him into the kid's room, shutting the door.

Meanwhile, Sulley charged through the factory until he reached the secret passageway. Growling ferociously, he ripped the tool panel off the wall and ducked inside. He ran through a maze of pipes and rooms, searching for Boo.

Suddenly he heard Boo whimper. Sulley ran towards the sound. Boo was already in the secret lab. Randall had strapped her to a chair in front of the extraction machine. Waternoose was watching. 'I never should have brought you in on this. Because of you, I had to banish my top Scarer,' he told Randall.

'Ah, Sullivan got what he deserved,' said Randall.

Fungus set the dial on the control panel. The machine revved up.

Boo's brown eyes grew wide with terror as the scream extractor moved closer and closer to her face. Opening her mouth, she began to scream.

'ROARRR!' Sulley cried, running towards the sound.

The machine was only an inch from Boo's face when Sulley burst into the lab, roaring like a thousand lions. He smashed the machine out of the way. It skidded across the floor and hit Fungus and Waternoose, pinning them against the wall. Sulley ran to the chair and released Boo.

'Kitty!' she cried happily.

'Stop him!' Waternoose yelled. Randall growled and chased after them.

Just as Sulley reached the exit, he was

hit in the face by something invisible. Two more invisible punches sent him reeling. Suddenly Randall unblended from the wall. 'You don't know how long I've wanted to do that, Sullivan,' he said. With a whip of his tail, he sent Sulley flying out into the Monsters, Inc. hallway.

Sulley wobbled to his feet – only to get hit in the face with a snowball! There, right in front of him, was Mike!

'Look,' Mike told him. 'It's not that I don't care about the kid!'

Sulley looked over his shoulder. Randall would be there any second. 'Mike, you don't understand . . .' he began. But before he could finish, the invisible Randall slammed him against the wall.

Unaware that his friend was being pummelled, Mike continued his speech. 'I was just mad, that's all! I needed some time to think. But you shouldn't have left me out there!'

'I'm being attacked!' Sulley gasped.

'No, I'm not attacking you,' Mike said. 'I'm trying to be honest. Just hear me out.'

Boo hurried to Mike's side and tugged at his arm. She pointed to Sulley, whose head suddenly jerked back. Randall was trying to strangle him!

But Mike still didn't get it. 'Oh, come on, pal,' he said, starting to get choked up. 'If you start crying, I'm gonna cry. I'm sorry I wasn't there for you.'

Sulley gasped, flailing his arms and legs. Mike was annoyed. 'Hey, I am baring my soul here. The least you could do is pay attention!' He hurled his last snowball at Sulley's head. Sulley managed to duck, and the icy missile hit Randall in the face. Randall stumbled backwards. Sulley took his chance and punched him hard.

When Randall hit the wall, he returned to his normal colour. 'Hey, look at that,' Mike said. 'It's Randall!'

Suddenly he realized what had happened. 'Ohhhhhh.'

Sulley grabbed Mike and Boo and took off running.

'Get up!' Waternoose, who was still stuck behind the machine, shouted at Randall. 'There can't be any witnesses!'

Meanwhile, the trio was charging down the hallway. 'I'm glad you came back,' Sulley told Mike as they sprinted along.

'Hey, somebody has to take care of you – you big hairball,' Mike said. He turned to glance back over his shoulder – and gasped.

Celia, her snakes flowing wildly, leapt through the air. With a warlike whoop, she tackled Mike!

'Schmoopsie-Poo!' Mike cried. 'I really can't talk!'

Sulley grabbed Mike's arm and started to drag him away. 'Come on!' he said.

But Celia wasn't going to be left behind this time. Holding tight to Mike's leg, she got dragged along, too. 'Michael, if you don't tell me what's going on right now, we are through!' she yelled.

Neither Sulley nor Celia was letting go. Mike was getting stretched like a rubber band. 'OK, here's the truth,' he said. 'You know the kid that they're looking for? Sulley let her in! We tried to send her back, but Waternoose has a secret plot and now Randall's behind us and he's trying to kill us!'

Celia gasped. 'You expect me to believe that pack of lies, Mike Wazowski?'

Just then the hood covering Boo's face fell backwards. 'Mike Wazowski!' she said. Surprised, Celia let go.

'I love you, Schmoopsie-Poo!' Mike called back to her as Sulley pulled him along.

CHAPTER 16

Mike, Sulley and Boo ran on to the Scare Floor. Mike swiped a card key in a door station and they waited anxiously for the door to appear.

Randall and Fungus were right behind them. 'There they are!' Randall cried. But suddenly a voice crackled over the intercom system. 'Attention, employees. Randall Boggs has just broken the all-time scare record!'

Before Randall and Fungus could take another step, they were surrounded by a crowd of excited monsters. The crowd cheered and tossed them in the air.

Nearby, Celia hung up the intercom phone and smiled.

The crowd slowed Randall down for a while, but not quite long enough. Sulley gasped as the lizard monster charged towards them. Thinking quickly, he hit the keypad. The door that had been about to drop into the station suddenly reversed and began to head back into the door vault.

'Grab on, Mike!' Sulley shouted. Holding Boo in one hand, Sulley grabbed a rising door with the other. Mike clung to his tail. The three sailed into the air – up and out of Randall's reach.

Inside the door vault, millions of doors on conveyor belts stretched as far as the eye could see. Mike, Boo and Sulley screamed as the door they were riding dropped steeply into the vault.

Suddenly Mike cried out, 'There it is!' Just ahead on the track was Boo's door!

But before they could reach it, Boo's

door split off on to a different track and began to move away from them.

Their own door began to slow down. Mike looked ahead and gulped. 'This is a dead end, Sulley,' he said. Turning to look behind them, they saw Randall riding towards them on another door. It looked like a dead end, indeed!

Then Sulley had an idea. 'Make Boo laugh!' he told Mike. They could use the power to activate the doors!

'What?' Mike said, confused.

'Just do it!' Sulley cried. Reluctantly Mike poked himself in the eye. Boo gave a big belly laugh.

As Boo's laughter echoed through the vault, the lights on all the doors lit up! Just as Randall was about to reach them, the three friends opened a door and jumped into the human world. They ended up in a house on a beautiful sandy beach.

'Come on!' said Sulley. 'We've got to find another door.' Dashing into another house, they found a closet and opened the door. They were back in the vault, standing in a doorway thousands of feet in the air. Door after door stretched below them. Boo's door was stopped just ahead. Carefully they began to make their way towards it.

But Randall was right behind them! Entering and exiting through different doors, Sulley, Mike and Boo jumped in and out of the human world, with Randall hot on their trail.

'Jump!' Mike said to Sulley, opening a door and waving his buddy through. 'I'm right behind you!' Just as Randall reached the door, Mike slammed it in his face.

'I hope that hurt!' Mike yelled as he jumped on to a moving door right behind Sulley and Boo.

'Great job, buddy. I think we lost him,' Sulley said. But he spoke too soon. Suddenly Randall appeared next to them and leaped on to their door. He snatched

Boo out of Sulley's arms with his tail. The little girl screamed.

'Boo!' cried Sulley. At that moment, Randall yanked out the pin that held Mike and Sulley's door to the track. The door began to fall.

'Nice working with ya!' Randall said with a sneer. Mike and Sulley's door plummeted into the vault. Randall took off with Boo tucked under his arm.

'Get it open!' Sulley cried as the door sailed through space.

'I'm trying!' Mike said, tugging at the doorknob. At last the door opened. Mike jumped through. Sulley followed him and shut the door in the nick of time. The door hit the ground and smashed into pieces.

A door opened in another part of the vault. Sulley and Mike stood in the doorway. They breathed a sigh of relief. That was a close one!

Just then, in the distance, Sulley spotted Randall! Sulley climbed up to the top of the door he and Mike were riding on. Following Sulley's lead, Mike jumped on to another door. *'Aaaahh!'* he screamed. The two friends took off, flying along the track at breakneck speed.

'Looks like we caught the express, pal!' Mike exclaimed.

In no time they caught up with Randall and Boo. But just as Sulley was about to grab him, Randall leaped through the door he was riding. Sulley followed them into a kid's bedroom.

'Boo!' Sulley cried. He hurried towards his little friend, who stood on the other side of the room. But before he could reach her, Randall tackled him. Sulley fell out of the open door. Dangling thousands of feet in the air, Sulley clung to the door frame with one hand.

'You've been number one for too long,' Randall shouted at Sulley. 'Now your time is up. And don't worry, I'll take good care of the kid.' Randall began to peel Sulley's fingers off the door.

Suddenly Randall screamed in pain! Boo had climbed on to his back and was pulling on his head fronds! As Randall struggled to get her off, Sulley climbed back into the room. He grabbed Randall by the neck.

Boo babbled something to Sulley. He put his face up close to Randall's. 'She's not scared of you any more,' he told the monster. 'Looks like you're out of a job.' Boo growled in agreement.

Nearby, Mike held up a door. 'All right, Sulley. Over the plate. Let's see the old stuff, pal. Here's the pitch . . .' Sulley wound up and threw Randall through the door like a baseball. 'And he is . . . outta here!' Mike cried, slamming the door behind him.

Randall landed in the closet of a house in the middle of a swamp. A little boy saw him.

'Mama!' the boy called. ''Nother 'gator

got in the house.'

''Nother 'gator?' the boy's mama said. 'Go get the shovel.'

'Ooph!' Randall grunted as the boy clobbered him on the head with a shovel.

'Get back here,' the boy said, swinging the shovel again.

Meanwhile, Mike lifted the door to the edge of the platform and pitched it over the edge. The door sailed into the vault and smashed into pieces. Randall was gone – for good.

CHAPTER 17

Sulley, Mike and Boo heaved sighs of relief. Then Boo babbled and pointed to something. The two monsters turned around. Boo's door was travelling by on a nearby track! They ran to it and grabbed on.

'OK, Boo,' Sulley told the little girl. 'It's time to go home. Take care of yourself and be a good girl.' But when he opened the door, all they saw was the vault whizzing by. The door had run out of power.

'Make her laugh again,' Sulley told Mike.

'All right, I've got a move that will bring

down the house,' Mike said. He jumped in the air and did a graceful flip. But then he lost his footing and landed upside down! There was no response.

Sulley looked down. Boo's hood was covering her eyes. 'Oh, sorry. She didn't see that,' he said.

Mike was angry that he'd hurt himself for no reason. 'What did you do? Forget to check if her stupid hood was up, you big dope?' he yelled at Sulley.

Boo didn't like to see Mike yelling. She began to frown.

Sulley noticed. 'Uncle Mike, try not to yell in front of her. You know we still need her to laugh,' he said in a singsong voice.

'Hey, Boo, just kidding,' Mike said. He poked himself in the eye. 'Ow! Funny, right?' But Boo was in no mood to laugh now.

Suddenly Boo's door jerked to the side. It began to move away from the other doors.

'Whoa! What's happening?' Mike cried.

'Hold on!' Sulley yelled.

It was Waternoose! He was still determined to make certain no one found out about his evil plan. He stood on the Scare Floor, waiting for Boo's door. 'When the door lands in the station, cut the power,' he told a worker standing at a power switch.

Sulley and Mike peeped out from behind the door as it moved towards the Scare Floor. Waternoose and a team of CDA agents waited for them.

'What are we gonna do?' Mike whispered.

The door landed. CDA agents crept forward. 'Come out slowly with the child in plain sight,' said an agent.

Mike appeared at the door, carrying Boo. 'OK, you got us. Here we are. Here's the kid. I'm co-operating. But before you take us away, I have one thing to say.' Mike stuck out his big tongue. It had a child's sock on the end! 'Catch!' he shouted, throwing the sock right on to an agent.

The frightened agents scattered to avoid the sock. In the meantime, Mike dashed off. The agents chased after him.

'Don't let them get away!' called Waternoose.

Waternoose began to follow Mike when he suddenly heard a noise. Turning around, he saw Sulley and Boo! Mike didn't have the kid after all! He just had her costume. She was with Sullivan! Waternoose called to the CDA agents, but they were already gone. The mean monster's eyes narrowed. He would have to take matters into his own claws.

With Boo under one arm and her door under the other, Sulley raced down the hall. Waternoose scuttled close behind. When he reached the simulator room, Sulley ran inside. He tore a pipe off the wall and jammed it through the door handles. And just in time! Waternoose banged against the door.

With each shove, Waternoose opened the doors a little further. Meanwhile, Sulley was desperately trying to get Boo's door into place in the station. Finally the door locked into position. Sulley dashed through.

When the monstrous crab burst into the room, he saw Sulley bent over Boo's bed, tucking her under the covers. Sulley looked up and gasped. 'She's home now. Just leave her alone!' Sulley pleaded.

'I have no choice!' Waternoose cried. 'Times have changed. Scaring isn't enough any more.'

'But kidnapping children?' said Sulley.

'I'll kidnap a thousand children before I let this company die!' Waternoose roared. 'And I'll silence anyone who gets in my way!' He lunged forward, pushing Sulley to the floor. Then he grabbed the child from her bed.

But it wasn't Boo. It was the puppet doll from the training-room! The bedroom walls began to rise into the air.

'Simulation terminated. Simulation terminated,' said the computerized voice.

Waternoose blinked in the bright lights. Then his eyes grew wide with shock. The simulator room was filled with CDA agents!

Mike was sitting in Ms Flint's chair. 'Well, I don't know about the rest of you guys,' he said to the agents, 'but I spotted several big mistakes. Let's watch my favourite part again.' He rewound the videotape. Waternoose appeared on the monitor. 'I'll kidnap a thousand children before I let this company die . . . I'll kidnap a thousand children before I let this company die . . .' he repeated again and again as Mike replayed the tape.

While the agents listened, Boo peeked out from under the bed, where she was hiding. 'Boo!' she said. Sulley put his finger to his lips so Boo would be quiet.

The CDA agents moved forward and grabbed Waternoose. As they led him out of the room, Waternoose shouted at Sulley, 'I hope you're happy, Sullivan! You've destroyed this company! Monsters, Incorporated is dead! The energy crisis will only get worse. Because of *you*!'

Sulley was upset. He'd always been proud of working for Monsters, Inc. He certainly hadn't meant for this to happen.

The head CDA agent stepped up to Sulley. 'Stay where you are,' he commanded. 'Number One wants to talk to you.' Sulley and Mike were confused. Who was Number One?

Two agents walked through the door. Then they stepped apart, revealing ...

'Roz?' Sulley and Mike exclaimed. Their dispatcher was actually the top CDA agent!

Roz slithered towards them. 'Two and a half years of undercover work were almost wasted when you intercepted that child, Mr Sullivan,' she said. 'Of course, without your help, I never would have known that this went all the way up to Waternoose.' She paused. 'Now, about the girl . . .'

Sulley scooped Boo into his arms. 'I just . . . want to send her home,' the big blue monster said sadly.

'Very good,' Roz said. 'Bring me a door shredder,' she ordered into a wrist communicator.

'You mean I can't see her again?' Sulley asked.

'That's the way it has to be,' Roz told him. 'I'll give you five minutes.'

CHAPTER 18

Sadly, Sulley inserted the card key in Boo's door. The red light above it blinked on.

Mike walked over to Boo to say good-bye. 'Well, so long, kid.'

'Mike Wazowski!' said Boo. She wrapped her arms around the green monster. Mike hugged her back. 'Yeah, it's been fun,' he said. 'Go ahead ... go grow up.'

When Boo turned around, she saw that Sulley had opened her door. The little girl squealed with delight and ran into her room. Taking Sulley by the hand, she led him around her room, showing him her favourite toys.

'Uh, Boo... Oh, look at that – that's cute,' Sulley said as she handed him one toy after another. 'Uh, Boo, well, that's very nice. Come here, you.' At last he picked her up and swung her over to her bed.

Boo looked at her closet. 'Nothing's coming out of the closet to scare you any more, right?' Sulley asked. Boo smiled and agreed. No more monsters in *her* closet!

Sulley leaned close to his little friend. 'Good-bye, Boo,' he said quietly.

'Kitty,' said Boo.

'Kitty has to go.' Sulley opened the closet door and stepped through. Slowly he closed the door behind him.

Boo waited on her bed for a minute. Then she jumped up and ran over to the closet. 'Boo!' she cried, throwing the door open wide.

But there was nothing inside her closet

but her clothes.

'Kitty?' Boo called out.

Back in the monster world, Sulley watched forlornly as two CDA agents put Boo's door through the shredder. Wood chips spewed out at the other end.

'None of this ever happened, gentlemen,' Roz said sternly as the shredder was wheeled away. 'And I don't want to see any paperwork on this.' Roz and the agents left.

Mike noticed a piece of Boo's door on the floor. He picked it up and handed it to Sulley. Sulley stared at it for a moment. Then he cradled it in his hand.

As they left the factory, Mike tried to cheer his buddy up. 'I'm telling you, pal, when that wall went up, you should have seen the look on Waternoose's face. I hope we get a copy of that tape!' Mike said. But Sulley just walked along with his head hanging down. 'Come on, pal, cheer up. We did it! We got Boo home!

Sure, we put the factory in the toilet, and . . . not to mention the angry mob that'll come after us when there's no more power. But hey, at least we had some laughs, right?'

As Mike continued to walk, Sulley slowed to a stop. 'Laughs?' he said. He was getting an idea!

CHAPTER 19

Moonlight streamed through the bedroom window. A little boy snuggled under the covers of his bed. Suddenly the door of his closet creaked open.

The boy gasped. Slowly a monster rose from beneath the bed. The boy was opening his mouth to scream ... when he was interrupted by a tapping sound.

'Is this thing on?' said a voice. 'Hello? Testing...'

The boy reached out and turned on his bedside lamp. A small, round, lime-green monster was sitting on a stool at the foot of his bed, tapping on a microphone.

'Hey, good evening! How are ya? It's great to be back here in . . . your room,' Mike said. 'You're in nursery school, right? I loved nursery school – best three years of my life.'

Mike paused, waiting for the kid to laugh at his joke. The kid didn't even crack a smile.

Mike tried again. 'But I loved sports! Dodge ball was the best. I was the fastest one out there. Course, I was the ball. Heh-heh.'

The kid just stared at Mike. Mike sighed. Suddenly he threw the microphone into his mouth and swallowed it. After making some loud stomach noises, he burped the microphone back out of his mouth.

'Ha ha ha!' the boy laughed, cracking up.

Mike caught the microphone and headed towards the closet door.

'Thanks a lot,' Mike said. 'I'll be here all week. Remember to tip your waitresses.'

Mike walked through the door . . .

. . . and on to the Scare Floor. Only it wasn't the Scare Floor any more. It was the Laugh Floor. Monsters, Inc. had made a few changes. Now all the power they collected came from kids' laughter!

Sulley applauded as Mike came through the door. 'Great job, Mikey. You filled your quota on the first kid of the day!'

'You know, only someone with perfect comedic timing could produce this much energy in one shot,' said Mike.

'Uh-huh,' Sulley said mischievously. He looked over at the new yellow canister attached to the door station. It was ten times bigger than the old scream canister. 'And the fact that laughter is more powerful than scream had nothing to do with it!' he declared.

'Oh, Googly Bear,' a voice called to Mike. 'Come here, you!'

'Schmoopsie-Poo!' Mike called back as he and Celia gave each other a big kiss. Celia's snakes kissed Mike too. Celia scolded the snakes, then smiled at Mike. 'Michael, you're such a charmer,' she said.

Sulley left the happy couple and made his way down the Laugh Floor. Everywhere workers stopped to greet him.

'Hey, President Sullivan,' replied a cheerful George. All his fur had grown back.

'Now, don't call me President. I'll start thinking I'm important,' Sulley said modestly. But Sulley *was* important. He had come up with the idea of using laughter instead of screams to power the city.

On the Laugh Floor, Sulley looked around, smiling. Everywhere laughter rose from doors and workers moved full laugh canisters. Business at Monsters, Inc. was better than ever, thanks to Sulley.

But Sulley's smile faded as he looked

down at his clipboard and lifted up several reports. There was the drawing that Boo had made of them together. Sulley still missed his little human friend.

Just then Mike came up to Sulley. He was holding something behind his back.

'Oh, hey, Mike. I was just, um...' Sulley said, quickly covering the drawing.

'Listen, if you got a minute, there's something I want to show you,' said Mike. 'OK, close your eyes. Follow me.'

He led Sulley to the simulator room. Sulley's eyes were closed. 'Keep coming, keep coming. Keep those eyes closed,' Mike instructed.

'Mike...' Sulley said, growing a little impatient. He took a few more steps.

'OK!' Mike said. 'Open 'em.' Sulley opened his eyes. There in front of him was Boo's door! Mike had carefully glued the whole thing back together.

The green monster smiled and held up his hands – they were covered in bandages from the splinters. 'Sorry it took so long, pal,' he said. 'There was a lot of wood to go through.'

Sulley stared at the door – one piece of wood was missing. 'It only works with every piece,' Mike told him. Sulley looked down at his clipboard, where he'd taped the piece of wood he'd saved from Boo's door. Picking it up, Sulley fitted it into the empty space.

The red light above the door blinked on. Nervously Sulley turned the handle . . . and peeked into Boo's room.

'Boo?' Sulley called out softly.

'Kitty!'

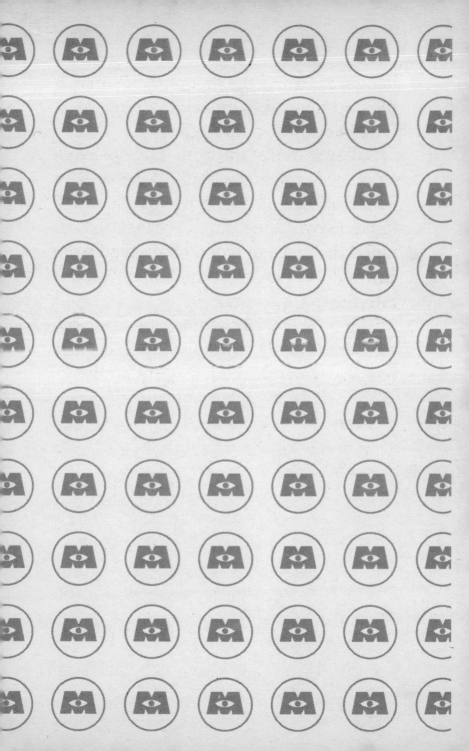

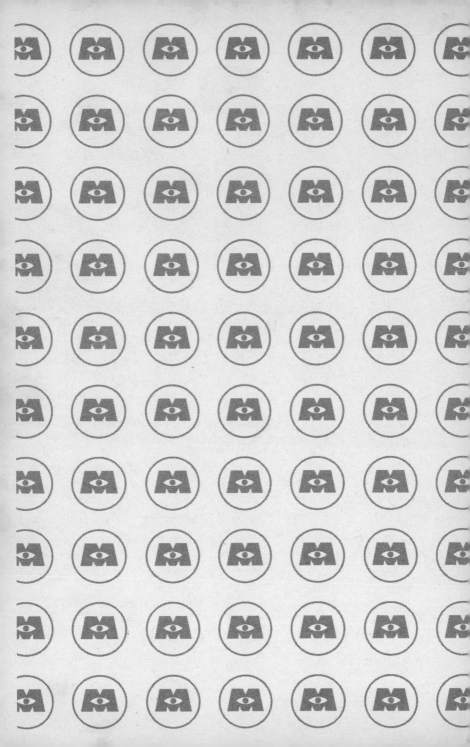